The Doggone Christmas List
and Other Stories

Robb Lightfoot

# The Doggone Christmas List

## and Other Stories

### Humor by
### Robb Lightfoot

Portions of this book appeared in
<u>The Funny Times</u>
and <u>aNewsCafe</u>

You may contact the publisher or the author at:
Or So It Seems Press
PO Box 214
Palo Cedro, CA 96073
<u>robb@orsoitseems.com</u>

ISBN: 0988785439
ISBN-13: 978-0-9887854-3-4

# ACKNOWLEDGEMENTS

I dedicate this book—my first—with gratitude to my wife, Karin for her constant support and encouragement through 30 years of friendship and marriage. Thanks, too, to my children, Amanda, Nicole, Rebecca and Joe, for allowing me to tell these tales—and not disowning me.

My work has been nurtured by my writing buddies, Charlie Price, Melinda Kashuba , Kathryn Gessner, Jim Dowling and Carla Jackson. I'm deeply indebted to you five for your sage advice and for sharing my joys and sorrows.

Publisher Doni Chamberlain also has been instrumental in getting my stories out into the world. Thank you for your encouragement and support.

Finally, I must give a nod to author, teacher and friend Tony D'Souza. For most of my career, I've labored in solitude and never sought "first readers" prior to sending out my work. Tony told me something that changed everything about how I write. Tony said "no one does it alone." This one tip opened my world to collaboration, the fellowship of serious writers, and publication.

This book would not exist without all these friends and my family.

# CONTENTS

## PREFACE

*This introduction appeared at the launch of my column, Or So It Seems....*

**Tall Tales and Tedious Trips – Welcome to Or So It Seems....**

I come from a family that loves good stories. When I was a kid, at our dinner table, everyone talked about their day, usually all at the same time. We'd take turns topping one another. There was lots of love, some shouting, laughter, and many a memorable tale. Some of the stories even had the added advantage of being true. Dinner guests who were first-time visitors were often taken aback until they learned to just wade in.

At grade school, I would talk up a storm, retelling these stories, shouting out answers to the teachers' questions, and filling in the punch lines to other people's jokes. I wanted attention, and I got it. Lots. I was given my own special reserved-seating desk in the principal's office. My first-grade teacher had a stack of referral slips with my name dittoed on them, and the box "talking in class" checked off. I remember this, and it may have actually happened….

So I survived school and, oddly enough, ended up back in the classroom. I make my living by forcing other people to talk in class—I'm a speech teacher. My subjects include how to overcome fear—hint, talk a lot—and research methods. In fact, I'm all for facts. But I also cover storytelling, too. And I know that a good story sometimes wanders into the land of the tall tale.

Fiction reveals the truth by telling a compelling story. But even non-fiction narratives offer conflicting views of reality. My graduate thesis was a study of "competing political narratives." I examined two stories where the heroes and villains were reversed and each side wanted to win to gain a big hunk of real estate. Who or what to believe? It's hard to know sometimes.

When my children were small, we'd pass the time on long trips by telling original, convoluted stories. It worked like this. My wife, Karin, or I would begin the yarn, and after a few paragraphs—a chapter—hand it off to one of the kids. The new narrator would pick up the thread and go on. The story would unravel as it moved around the van. By the time it made it back to me, the plot was a hopeless tangle. How? Why? Who knew?

Sometimes, when we were overdue for a rest stop, a back-seat troll might kill off my favorite character. One time this happened, just as the story-telling-staff was passed back to me, and I decided a case of literary CPR was in order. I revived my character, Wilbur.

A howl arose from the back seat.

"You can't do that," the Greek chorus said.

"Do what?" I replied in innocence.

"Bring back Wilbur."

"But he's not really dead".

"They found his body floating in the lake," my daughter Amanda said.

"Or so it seemed...." I said. "Later tests proved it wasn't him".

My daughter fumed. "So who was it?"

"Don't know." I shrugged.

Somehow, this answer didn't satisfy Amanda, She'd taken a personal dislike to Wilbur. All my heroes were named Wilbur, and she'd apparently had enough of them.

So when the story circled back around to her, she sought her own revenge. Wilbur was about to get married... a happy ending was in view. And then Amanda struck.

"But the police arrested Wilbur and threw him in jail. He was convicted of murder and executed," Amanda said.

"Hey," I protested, "Why would they do that?"

"Because it was someone impersonating Wilbur," she said.

"But the tests proved it wasn't."

"Or so it seemed," she said. I saw her smile in my rear-view mirror. "But the Wilbur-impersonator snuck into the lab and changed the test tubes."

"How did they know?" I asked.

"He left a fingerprint on the test tube, and a brilliant investigator named Amanda figured it out," she said. "The end."

And that was when the "Or So It Seems" method of storytelling entered our family history. At least that's how I remember it. It could have happened this way. Or not.

You'll have to ask Amanda.

.

Robb Lightfoot

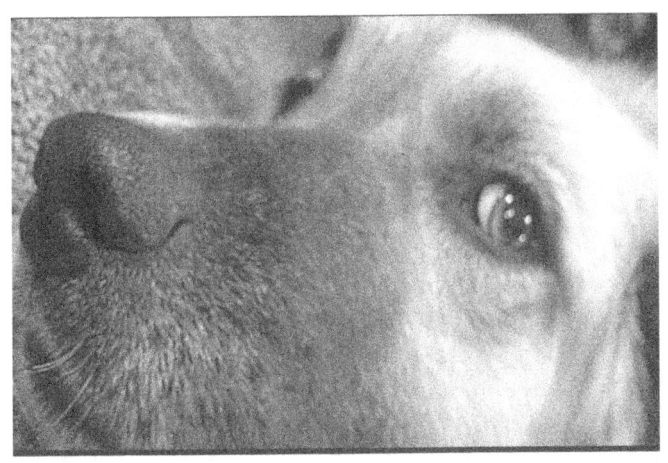

# THE DOGGONE CHRISTMAS LIST

I'm working on "The Christmas List," and I can see Lucy, my wife's dog, watching me.

Now Lucy's a pretty smart pooch. She knows that when I put her on the leash, it's time to go to the vet. Usually, on Lucy's morning walks, my wife does the honors. But when it's just me, Lucy dutifully plods straight to the car rather than barreling down the driveway. She knows what's up.

So it's entirely possible that she sees "The List" and grasps its significance in just the same way that she understands the sound of food rattling into her bowl, or the sight of my wife pulling on running shoes before a walk.

I ponder, and Lucy comes over. Big brown eyes look deeply into mine, and she puts her Anatolian-Shepherd head on my knee. Maybe she's been reading my mind. It's been a tough year, and I'm wondering just how generous I can afford to be. Most of the kids are out of the house, so the fussing volume has subsided over the years. I can stop and reflect on the economics of gift-giving. Maybe I can dial it back a bit, but then there's this dog and its sustained stare.

I try to remember what the dogs got last Christmas. They have their own stockings, of course, and I seem to recall that they had a better year, stocking-wise, than I did. Not that I'm jealous or anything. I don't know that I really wanted jerky, a leather chew bone, or the studded collar. Well, not the chew bone anyway....

But the budget? Maybe I could kill a tradition, and hide the animals' stockings in the ornament box, buried under that hideous blue-and-green wreath. The wreath is another tradition, an heirloom given to us by a fashion-impaired relative. We never use it. I dare not give it away, and so it sits in the bottom of the box, year after year. This is, I think, the perfect hiding place. But, then, I'd have to explain to the wife why I neglected the critters. Nope. Not a pretty picture.

I in my defense, I was in the pet store the other day. I got stocking-stuffer shock. Even the cheap stuff seemed to be at least $5 a throw, or more. Then I did the math. You have to get each animal at least two--I think that's in the US Constitution somewhere. And it's not just the dogs, even the naughtiest cats get them. The expenses all add up.

Way, way up,

That's how things tend to happen around here. With four kids, pets for each of them, and a wife who never met a dog she didn't like, we're pushing double digits. The funny thing is that when the kids moved away, the animals remained. I'm not just talking about the ones buried in the back yard, I'm talking about the ones that are still walking around here, chewing up the upholstery and eating the houseplants.

A small voice in my head says, "Can't we start being practical?" Would they furry ones really miss being crossed off "The List?" I can definitely cut the cats. What would they care? Every day must seem like Christmas. Turn your back, and they're up on the counter feasting away. And doesn't it set a bad example to have them all jacked-up on catnip while we gather around the tree?

This is beginning to sound almost convincing, and then Lucy leans against me and sighs. She sounds, well, disappointed. My inner Scrooge misses a step. I absently stroke her fur, coarse and fuzzy at the same time, and I wonder…. What DO we owe our pets? I look at Lucy and reflect on what she means to my wife, and to all of us. It has been a tough year, and more than once, hugging that silly dog was the high point of someone's day, even mine.

This explains why Lucy will stay on "The List." After all, she is almost-well-behaved, better than me, really. Besides, I don't think I could face those eyes on Christmas day and have Lucy wonder why Santa forgot her. I pencil in her name. Just then, she licks me, wags her tail, and saunters away. I hear her toenails clicking down the hallway, and the room is still.

So much for the budget. Maybe she'll share the jerky.

## BETTER FUSSING
## IN 5 MINUTES A DAY

Hey, kids. Christmas is coming up, and it's time to work up your Santa-list and the even longer one for your parents. As a reformed child, I know that getting what you want requires determination and lack-ofdiscipline. Here are keys to the kingdom of fussing, gained from many years of watching my kid sister in action and a few tricks of my own. Use them in good health, unless you're related to me. In which case, quit reading immediately and go mow the lawn.

## Delivery Checklist

Fussing skills are innate but peak in early childhood. Fortunately, you can emulate a 4-year-old to good effect no matter what your age. Watch for a free refresher course in your neighborhood grocery store's candy aisle. Observe the following:

✓ Select the perfect pitch. Whining is crucial. Practice upward inflection at the end of sentences until you reach the hyper-sonic range of dog whistles. If Rover runs for cover, you're almost there.

✓ Breath control. You have choices here. Gasping is good, but staccato bursts of random sounds are more irritating. Amplitude is everything. In public places, you can generate more noise than a 747. Practice. Holding vowels for 2-12 minutes is possible with a lungful of air. Try this. See how long you can sustain the "OM" sound when saying MOOOOOOOOOOOM.

✓ Repetition. It's hard to ignore what goes on for a half hour. "Mother. Mommy. Momma. Mom. Ma. " punctuated by repeated pokes to the ribcage are guaranteed to get some sort of reaction.

✓ Mask    semi-obnoxiousness with manners. "Please" is one of the magic words, remember?

✓ Putting it all together. "Ah, Ah, PLEEEASE MOM." (Gasp) "I'll BEEEE SOOOO GOOOOD THIS TIME." (Whimper.) "Mommy. Mom. *Mother*." (Poke. Poke. Poke.) "PLEEEEEEEASE!" (Sound of shattering glass.)

## Applied Psychology

In addition to HOW you beg, WHEN and WHERE matter greatly.

### ASKING MOM – Five Easy Steps

Try these five easy steps, and watch your success rate climb!

1. Put your target in the right frame of mind. For Mom, this means doing the dishes or sweeping the floor without being asked. Bigger requests entail random acts of mopping, and desperate,    over-the-top    demands

mean tangoing with the toilet brush. And we're not talking about a mess y*ou* made. This is owning *SOMEONE ELSE'S CLEANUP CATASTROPHE*. Be careful here. If the room was tidy the last time Mom saw it, then it doesn't count. You have to make sure she saw your little sister's effort to feed pancakes to Barbie. Rat her out if necessary.

2. Timing matters. Avoid first thing in the morning bedside-begging, when she's trapped-behind-the-wheel-wheedling or lights-out-at-nighttime-niggling. You'll be ignored. Forgo any attempts when Mom is expecting her co-workers, boss, or other "visiting royalty." Ditto the surprise arrival of any white-haired or wrinkled relative.

3. Make eye contact—you've got to have her full attention. It's OK to tug on Mom's blouse when she's talking, if she's only babbling to herself. Don't try it when she's changing a diaper, on the phone, cooking, cleaning or doing all that stuff Moms seem to think are more important than listening to you. Don't try to do anything through a closed door, especially the bathroom door. IMPORTANT! If you hear her singing or humming a tune, IMMEDIATELY

drop whatever you're doing and hit her with your biggest demand.

4. Good salesmanship begins with a big smile and tons of confidence. Let the enthusiasm just ooze out of your voice. Dash into the room, throw your arms open wide and announce: "Mom, I've got a great idea... Can I..." The idea may not, in fact, be all that great. And don't ask if *SHE* thinks it's a great idea. The point is that you've got to sell it to her, big and fast. Don't lose heart. Remember, this is the woman whose mother, Grandma, bought the entire set of *World Books* on the installment plan, from the door-to-door encyclopedia salesman, *AND IS STILL GETTING THE YEARBOOKS*.

5. Become a student of nonverbal communication. If you have a compound-complex, multiple-part fuss, then you need to learn when to quit. If her smile begins to flatten, or you see creases at the corners of the eyes that weren't there when you started, desist. If she shrugs or mumbles something through a mouthful of bobby pins, assume the answer was YES! Bolt from the room before she can clarify, and then remind her later that "*you promised*."

## ASKING DAD – Sure-fire Pointers

With Dad, concentrate on this one, proven technique.

➢ Study TV listings. Find when his favorite program airs.

➢ Hide the remote so he can't pause the show or turn up the volume.

➢ Thirty seconds before kickoff, drag his toolbox in.

➢ Hover between him and the screen.

➢ Begin with the phrase "Dad, can you help me..." Usually, you won't need to finish your sentence. But if he's a bit slow, drop some tools. Greasy ones first.

Nine times out of ten, you'll hear: "GO BOTHER YOUR MOTHER!"

Then, go to back to *Mom-Step-1*, adding, "Dad told me to ask you...."

# A THRIFT-SHOP HOLIDAY

I do holiday shopping year-round. When I'm on the road in a small town, I find treasures on the cheap, things you won't see at Sears.

So it was that I stepped into Deercreek Thrift, a Saturdays-only shop next to a trailer-camp, on a side-road miles from the Interstate. It has a warped door you tackle to open. Inside you'll find Doris, the proprietor. She's all of 4-foot-nothing, age ... between 80 and 200-hundred. Her face looks like it's been carved out of expired Velveeta.

An unseasonable cold snap had caught me unprepared, and I could see my breath as I walked into the store. First order of business—find a sweater.

I brushed by the counter, soiling my shirt.

"The dirt's free," Doris said.

A big man in a NASCAR shirt rubbed a beer stein on his chest.

"How much?" He asked.

"$2.62."

"If it said Germany or Bavaria on it, I'd pay 40 bucks."

Doris spoke again. "$3.62"

"It's a replica."

"If it wasn't, It wouldn't be $4.62."

"I liked the first price better."

"Shouldn't mouth-off."

A woman wearing hoop earrings elbowed beer-stein-man out of the way. She laid several sweaters on the counter and flapped her arms for warmth. Doris looked at the tags.

"That's $8.50," Doris said.

"The sign says $1 a bag."

"Oh... Yeah." Doris put the sweaters in a bag.

"That'll be $10."

The woman reddened. "I beg your pardon?"

"Sweaters are a buck. The bag's nine dollars."

The woman snatched the sweaters out of the sack and flung it on the floor.

"Watch it," Doris tapped her finger on a sign in the display case that read: "We reserve the right to refuse service to anyone."

The woman pursed her lips, pulled out a $10 bill, and waited for Doris to make change. Doris returned six quarters, and re-bagged the sweaters. Hoop-earring-woman snatched the bundle and stalked off.

Maude, one of Doris' helpers, trudged up carrying a big box.

"Same gal from last year," Doris said.

"Yep. I remember," Maude said.

"Didn't learn from the experience."

"No manners," Maude shook her head. She perched the box on her hip. It was crammed with books, stacked so that you couldn't see the title of anything but the top one. She worked her way around a white-haired man, and plunked the box down in a chair in front of the book case, blocking all the titles.

The man grunted. "Hey, I can't see what's in the mystery section."

"Kind of appropriate." Doris saw I was watching and winked.

"How the hell do you expect to sell anything that way?"

"Oh, I don't. But pretty soon you'll be moving boxes and chairs. Then you'll be working here for free."

The man didn't smile.

"Where's that John le Carre' book I was gonna buy?"

"Sold it," Doris said.

"Told you I was going to buy it."

"Put any money on the counter?"

"Had to go back to my trailer."

"That was last week."

I chuckled, and Doris seemed pleased. The man turned on me, frowning.

"You got my book there?"

"No," I said, taking a step backward. "Just a couple of children's books." I had yet to find a sweater.

The man came at me, staring down at my pending purchases.

"Ursula Le Guin," he said. "Who the hell is that?"

"An award-winning author," I said.

"She a Commie?"

"Hell, Mike, you think all writers are Red."

I took this break to edge away, and retreated into the store. It was more disorganized than the front, video cassettes stacked on end, facing backwards amid racks of clothing for $2 a bag, "half-off through the end of the month." The sign looked pretty beat, and it was only the third of June.

"Are the clothes still half-off?" I shouted.

"Read the sign," Doris said.

"Well, that's what it says. I thought that maybe you were confused."

There were shuffling and scurrying sounds. A moment later, Doris appeared. Her jaw was set, and her eyes glittered. She seemed to have grown a foot or two.

"The sign says 'half price,' right?"

I gulped. "Yes ma'am."

"Then that's the deal, sonny, unless you want to pay full price."

"OK. OK. But the sign looks like it's been up there a while.

"You're a genius, Sherlock."

"The end of the month?"

"Each and every month. Kind of hurries people along." The wrinkles were moving into a new configuration. A scowl? A smile? Who can tell?

"Conversation starters," she said. "Gives the campers something to talk about when they get home. No one else comes through here." The front door slams, and Doris and scoots back to her perch, leaving me alone in the chaos.

Deercreek Thrift, I decide, is less a store than a landfill guarded by a geriatric gargoyle.

I've yet to find a sweater, but hiding in a corner I spy a velvet-Elvis. Perfect for aunt Barbara's Nashville shrine.

You can't find *that* at Sears.

I wonder if it's a replica.

## LETTERS TO SANTA

Dear Santa:

Do you really read all the letters people send to you?

I was listening to "Santa Claus Is Coming To Town..." It says that you're making a list, and checking it twice. How come? Do we get a second chance if we just happened to get blamed for something that no one really saw us do?

Dad says I'm getting a stocking full of coal this year, and it'll be a hot day at the North Pole before I see an electric train under the tree. Please prove Dad wrong on account of Global Warming melting the ice caps. Write soon, before the stores sell out.

Ronnie

*DEAR RONNIE:*

*I'm quite busy, but I did get your letter. Fortunately for us, it's always cold at the North Pole. But I can tell you that you won't get coal this year. I'm reducing my carbon footprint.*

*I haven't checked a second time—yet. But I do recall that you're not on the "good" list so far. You THOUGHT no one was watching, but the Santa Surveillance Cam saw what you did to Mr. Whiskers. It's not nice to tie raw bacon to a string and feed it to your neighbor's cat.*

*Tell your parents, and apologize, and I'll see what I can do. Clean your slate before the second review.*

*Merry Christmas and good luck.*

*Santa*

Dear Santa:

Wow. You really _are_ watching all the time. OK. I can tell Mom, but what about Dad? He'll kill me. My friend Leonard actually tied the bacon on the string, I just pulled it out. In my defense, the cat was still happy to eat it a second time. And does Mom need to know about the paint can falling off the roof? They've almost forgotten and blamed it on the repairman anyway.

What's the best way to apologize for something when it's only half your fault?

Ronnie


_DEAR RONNIE:_

_Apologies usually begin with "I'm sorry," and they work better if you mean it._

_Yes, I wondered if you were going to fess up to the splatter-painted sidewalk. You need to level with your folks. In fact, I have your file in front of me, and you've got a good bit of Smoothing over to do._

_But take heart, Christmas is a time of forgiveness and good will towards men... and energetic boys. Part of growing up, and getting big-kid toys, is doing the right thing, even when it's hard. Parents can be forgiving. Try it._

*Let me know how it works out. There's a big-league-slugger bat in it for you.*

*Santa*

Dear Santa:

Well, I did it. I told Mom. *She* shouted, cried and pouted. But I'm still alive—barely. I told her about almost everything, except for the home-made blowtorch. Just because I TOLD Leo how to build one, and he DID it, doesn't make it my fault, right? I figure you can talk to him about that one, OK?

No one's noticed the scorched cushions on the lawn furniture. Maybe you can bring Mom some new ones?

And Leo's not speaking to me because Mom told his dad about the bacon and the other stuff you already know about

Ronnie

P.S. – Leo thinks I'm making this up just to get him in trouble for a change. He NEVER gets caught.

*DEAR RONNIE AND LEO:*

*Friends don't let friends burn lawn furniture. You two need to sort this out.*

*Ronnie, You're on the right track,, but I think your mother deserves something better than replacement cushions. Don't you?*

*Leo, I'm waiting to hear from you. There's more than just one list, you know, nice, naughty, and the Santa-Parent-Conference. Don't make me pull my sleigh over...*

*Only 12 days to Christmas, The elves are calling. Gotta fly.*

*Santa*


hey Santa:

If this is for real... It's just Ronnie's word against mine, and who you gonna believe? Bacon-boy or me?

OK. So he's fingered me for some stuff that he put me up to. Big deal. No witnesses, no crime I say.

I'd stay out of this, if I were you. Remember, my dad's an attorney.

Leo

*Dear Leo:*

*As the song says... "I know when you're awake." And Leo, I know when you've been smoking behind the boy's gym, too.... Play with fire, and you'll get burned.*

*Just finished the second list-checking.... Better luck next year.*

*Santa*

# FROM THE LAW OFFICE
# OF B. BURNS, ES

**Christopher Kringle, aka Santa Claus**

**c/o General Delivery, North Pole**

**RE: Demand letter for damages on behalf of my client Leo**

**Dear Mr Kringle:**

**I am directing you to cease-and-desist your slanderous allegations directed at my client, Leo Burns. Leo has experienced extreme emotional distress**

on account of your unfounded and unsubstantiated accusations.

We are seeking compensation on his behalf.

Also, it appears you're practicing psychiatry without a license, dispensing advice and peppermint, violating privacy laws, as well as transporting imported goods and wild animals without the required permits.

We're estimating the cost of Leo's pain and suffering.

We're open to an initial settlement offer and response from you. If we can expedite this and resolve the matter before Christmas, we could avoid contacting the authorities and complicating your Christmas plans, if you get my drift.

Respectfully,

B. Burns


DEAR MR BURNS:

Ah, like father, like son....

I see you haven't changed, Big-"B". Thanks to your thoughtful note, I've triple-checked the list. Here's Santa's settlement for the Bad-Burns-Boys.

Under the tree, Leo will find a box of nicotine patches and a fire extinguisher.

And for you, Big "B," since you still enjoy making a stink.... Check your yard for payment-in-full—a father-son gift of hand tools and two tons of reindeer droppings.

HOE-HOE-HOE.

Merry Christmas.

Santa

## NATIONAL FRUITCAKE MONTH
## A MAYAN WARNING

Every December, my wife and I clash on the most serious question of our time.

## Is fruitcake food or something far more sinister?

My wife belongs to a not-so-secret society that LIKES fruitcake. I find this troubling. To me, the stone-like substance masquerading as dessert is an evil recipe-gone-wrong. How is it possible to take so many tasty goodies and have them become a brick-like, molar-breaking mass. What dark forces are at work?

Let's look at ingredients in a typical recipe, such as Nicole Routhier's "Tutti-Frutti Fruitcake" at ingestandimbibe.com.

In alphabetical order, we begin with – *apples, apricots, peaches, pears, pineapples* and *raisins*.

Great so far. Apricots, eh? OK. But apples? APPLE PIE, APPLE SAUCE, CARAMEL APPLES.

Fantastic.

Peaches and pears? Individually or together, I'll take them whole, sliced, diced, in cobbler or in a pie.

Pineapples? Pizza isn't pizza without pineapples, and what's a good hike or camping trip without raisins?

What's next on Routhier's list? *Bourbon or dark rum*.

I'm not a Southerner, so I have no use for bourbon. But rum? Now you're talking, and the next thing on the list?

*Orange juice.* In the kitchen with rum and OJ! Why bother baking?

Now we run into trouble. *Cloves.* Really? Mixed with *fruit*? Cloven-evil, stay away from my stove!

Then what else gets tossed in?

*Eggs, flour, sugar, salt, baking soda.* Basic cake stuff. What could be wrong here? And then it's finished off with *almonds, butter, honey, and heavy cream.* Sounds wonderful, right?

It may look good on paper. But trust me, something possessed the dough in the darkness. It's hopeless—too much, too late. It's fruitcake.

Aficionados defend it, but fruitcake is the least-edible-food on the planet. How bad? Even bacteria won't touch it. Jay Leno once sampled a 125-year-old heirloom loaf, according to an article in the *Tuscaloosa News* of December '03.

"Needs more aging," Leno said. So the cake's caretakers rewrapped it in a rum-soaked-cloth, apparently to be brought out in another 125 years. No doubt, the show will be hosted by Jay.

Can't we just eat honey-roasted almonds? Or whip cream on peaches? *What compels people to make fruitcake*?

I took my question to *Wikipedia*, the infallible source on things the *Britannica* is afraid to print. In "Fruitcakes Found in Tut's Tomb," I learned ancient Egyptians thought the loaf-that-never-expires was necessary in the afterlife.

"Perhaps it was used for immortality," says Prof. I.N. Edible. No word yet on whether the Pharos used it to *enter* the afterlife. "It's true that some ancients committed suicide to pass into the next world, but toxicological studies of mummies are inconclusive on this point."

Inconclusive? Really? Were the mummies smiling? Or nonplussed? That ought to answer the question.

Fruitcakes may be timeless, but we know now they're deadly. How? Buried in a forthcoming *Journal of the American Fruitcake Society* scholarly article, I read a tale of invasion and cultural extermination. It's an eye-opener, and shows that we had it ALL WRONG about the history of Mexico.

## MAYAN—FRUITCAKE CONNECTION – UNEARTHED.

*"Code-breakers have debunked the Mayan-calendar-myth. From their efforts, and the seminal work of semi-journalists on Wiki-Leaks, We now know the story our government has been trying to silence. <u>Space aliens contacted the Mayans, gave them secrets of advanced mathematics, celestial mechanics, and, sadly, fruitcake technology."</u> JAFS 4-1-2012.*

The good news—The stone disk *doesn't* foretell the end of the world.

The bad news—It's a food warning–label chiseled on a granite-patty.

Think about it. Their "calendar" features a disgusted face. THEY WERE SENDING AN ALERT.

Don't believe me? Check it out yourself on the PFN - The Psychic Fruitcake Network at 1-800-I-WILL-SWALLOW-ANYTHING, extension 12-21. Hear the whole story for only $25 a minute.

So, no, I won't be eating fruitcake, even though ***December 27th is National Fruitcake Day.***

But if you get a fruitcake from some starry-eyed Mayan descendent... Fear not. Saturday, January 5th is "The Annual Great

Fruitcake Toss" in Colorado. For a small fee, you can hurl your unwanted, stone-like loaf into the void. You may even win a prize. The event is a popular tradition in Manitou.

I channeled event organizer Skip A. Stone. He claims that the annual gathering meets "a serious need... offering people a place to put that-which-no-landfill-wants." Skip denied rumors of an EPA shut-down."

"No way we're a Superfund-site." He shook his fist. "Fruitcake may be indestructible, but it's arguably organic." He pointed to a wall of recipes. "There's no evidence of PCBs, fluorocarbons, or nutritional content." Skip donned rubber gloves, grabbed tongs and lifted a cake for my inspection.

"See?" He thrust the loaf in my face. "The main ingredient is flour—a heated hydrocarbon. No worse than manure."

I flinched. He dropped the fruitcake on the counter. It landed with a thud.

"But *they* don't stink," Skip nodded in contemplation. "Mostly, they've got a nice, rummy smell."

"So, they're safe for human consumption?"

"Didn't say *that*." He shook his head. "Just nothin' illegal…. I think."

"Wasn't there an EPA complaint?" I asked.

He shrugged. "What're they gonna do? Nevada offered a fruitcake-disposal site. It bogged down in Congress."

Skip did concede the cakes can last for centuries, but he sees this as a plus.

"We thinking about making a Di-O-Rama, like that one in Disneyland," he said. "We'll call it *The American Fruitcake — A Retrospective*.

"Put up a ticket counter and a roof, and dig a trench." He leaned back I his chair and nodded. "Piece of cake. Just need a backhoe and dynamite."

He smiled.

"Lots of dynamite."

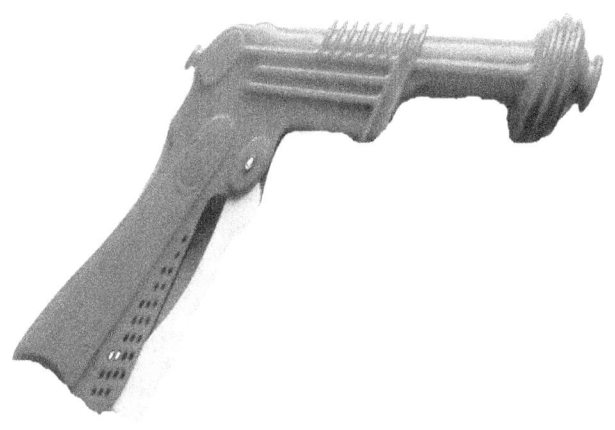

## THE RED PISTOL

Let me tell you about the first time I brought a gun into a bank.

Yes, I had Mom's permission, and it was only a water pistol. What possible trouble could a three-year-old have with just a water pistol, after all?

Mother soon found out.

Now, Mom was against the water-pistol idea from the start. But Dad bought it anyway, and it immediately became my favorite Christmas present. I carried it everywhere, and even slept with it. On that fateful Thursday, just after New Year's, she had a half-dozen errands to run and figured that it was best to keep me occupied. So, the red plastic pistol came with us. Better, she thought, to just let me keep it, and she took the precaution of emptying it.

I was totally absorbed with gunning down each and every teller, with a "kabang," "kabang," "kabang," and "click." Apparently, my water gun was a three-shooter. The tellers all smiled, and went about their business.

Mother patiently waited her turn in line, and wasn't concerned as I wandered about, hiding behind the potted palms and ducking under the new accounts desk. Mom was busy preparing her deposit and trying to roll some pennies while she juggled her checkbook and purse.

Gradually, I worked my way back over to my mother, and stood there next to her as the bank president walked up and greeted us.

"My, my, is this a holdup?" Mr. Stevens said to Mom, motioning toward me.

They both laughed, and then I squirted the banker right in his face, a dead-accurate shot.

"Oh, my," he said, reaching for his handkerchief, his eyes wide. Water dripped off his nose.

Mother looked at me and at my gun. She snatched it from my hands and saw that it was still half-full. "I'm so sorry, Mr. Stevens. This was empty." And then, Mom turned to me. "Where did you get water?"

I smiled, and pointed to a door--the men's room.

A more experienced mother might have known better, but since I was her first-born, she had to ask. "How did you reach the sink?"

"No." I shook my head. "Whoosh," I made a downward motion with my hand. "Water in potty seat."

Mr. Stevens finished mopping his face, and was about to put the handkerchief back in his pocket. Instead, he held it out gingerly with just two fingers, at arm's length, and walked briskly off to the restroom.

Mom lowered her head to avoid the stares of everyone within earshot, and kept her eyes down until we got through the line and exited the bank. Once on the street, she looked up, burst out laughing, and handed me back my pistol. "When we get home, show Daddy what you did today."

So I did.

Same water.

## FOOD FOLLIES
## THANKSGIVING LEFTOVERS
## **<u>EXPIRED</u>**

"Hey Dad. You gonna pack the potato salad?" My son pointed to a container on the kitchen counter. "It's been out all night."

I was the foreman on that day's lunch-assembly-line. We 're behind schedule, and I wasn't interested in quality-control.

"Probably."

"But it's got mayo?" He frowned.

"Yep."

"And mayo's made with eggs?" His voice trailed off.

"Right again." I said.

"Mr. Harvick, my life-skills teacher, says bad eggs make you sick."

"No problem." I winked. "These eggs graduated top of their class."

My son chewed on his lip. "I'll pass on the potatoes."

"Really, son? Who you going to believe? Him or me?"

"Well...."

I was crushed. It was one of those moments when you know that you're no longer the source-of-all wisdom for your child. True, I was stretching Thanksgiving leftovers well past the 12-Days-of-Christmas. But he'd never complained before.

"Tell you what. I'll bet you $5 it's OK."

"Five bucks?" My son's interest was revived.

"I'm eating it. And if I don't die, you owe me a fiver."

"But if you croak, how do I collect?"

I guess they don't teach compassion in life-skills.

But, *really*, how much should you worry about food safety? I'm living proof that the immune system is a thing of wonder. On the other hand, my wife, a nurse, is pretty careful. She throws things out that look *perfectly fine*. Just because they have "*expired*." In addition to the potato salad, I'm making myself a ham sandwich, and I offer her one.

"What's the date?" She asks.

I glance at my watch. "It's the 15th."

"NO. THE EXPIRATION DATE."

"Oh, I don't know." I looked at the torn wrapper and didn't see it.

"The ham's from the last Costco run," she says.

"If you say so."

"That was weeks ago." She shakes her head. "You really want food poisoning?"

I look at my sandwich. It looks harmless enough.

"Sam-I-Am ate ham that was green and lived," I said.

"Did you ever see him in a sequel?"

"Well... no," I admitted. So I turned the wrapper inside out, and found the magic numbers. "Looks like it's dated... yesterday."

"Is that the sell-by date or the use-by date?" She asked.

"Don't know."

"Then I wouldn't eat it." She warned.

"But it's yesterday. One day's growth is gonna kill me?"

"If it got left out..."

"It didn't." I said. But I couldn't be sure, not without watching the surveillance tapes. Maybe it had broken parole and made off with the mozzarella. My wife had planted the seed of doubt. So I went back to the fridge, the land of suspicious lunch meat, seeing if we had something else. "We've got some sliced chicken, fresh in the wrapper."

"Fresh? I don't remember buying it," she said.

"I think I did."

"Expiration?" She asked.

I looked on the wrapper. "Best by … last Tuesday."

"No thanks."

"Hey, it's unopened. No one left it out."

"It should have been used weeks ago."

"'Best by…' doesn't mean it will be bad."

"Mystery meat." She wrinkled her nose.

"It's chicken, not cafeteria food."

"No. Thank. You."

"I'll eat it."

"Then I'll visit you in the ER." She sighed, "Look. I can make my own sandwich."

"No," I said. "It's my turn and I'll do it."

"OK. Then just make me a peanut butter sandwich, please." She cocked her head. "And you have washed your hands…. Right?"

So I dug around in the cupboard and found a dusty peanut butter jar and a squeeze container of granulated honey. I waved them in her face. "This is what you want?"

"Please."

"But this stuff has been in there since Y2K." I said.

"It keeps."

"OK," I shrugged. "Dessert?"

"Maybe. What do we have?"

I checked the fridge, freezer and cookie jar. Nothing. Our daughter had cleaned out the fresh fruit.

I dug deep into the pantry, exploring shelves that I didn't know we had. There, hidden and forgotten, I found a relic of bygone era—an ancient package of Twinkies.

"Ooooh." I smiled, and tucked the treat in her lunch. "I found something special just for you."

"Thanks."

I handed her the bag.

"You'll like it." I kissed her on the cheek. "Doesn't expire until the year 2525."

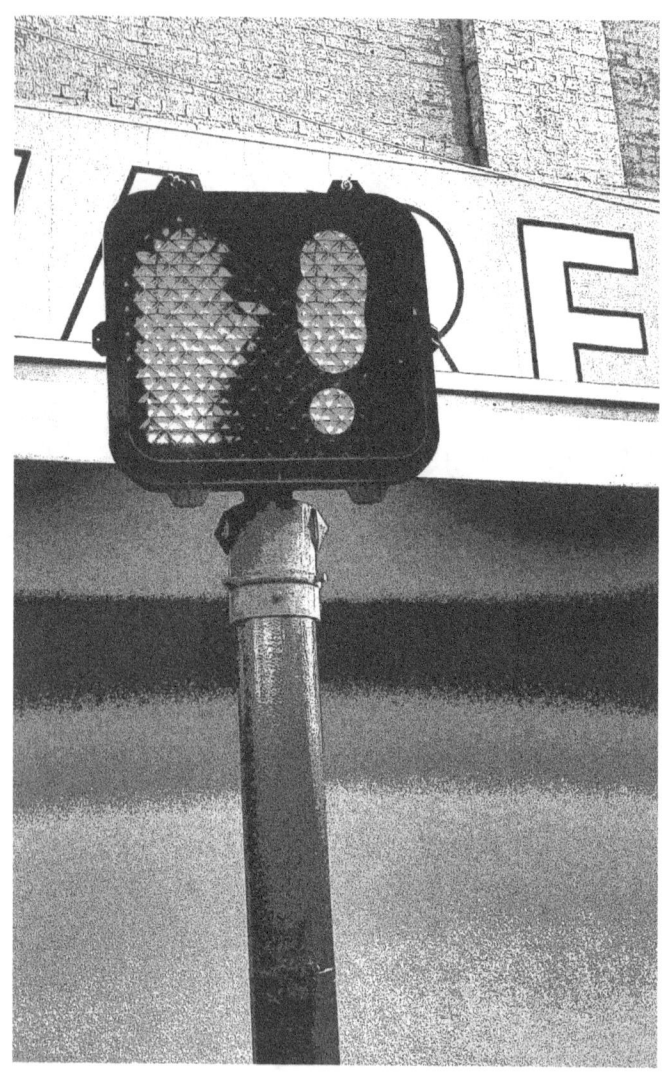

# SIGNS OF TROUBLE
# ON THE ROAD
# TO GRANDMOTHER'S HOUSE

The highlight of our Christmas vacation was when Mom and Dad packed our Pontiac station wagon and headed for Grandma and Grandpa's house. It was three days on the road, and Mom loaded the car with diversions—such as coloring books and road sign-bingo cards. But she knew that these wouldn't hold us for the entire trip. So, Mom made sure that we the seating strategy was designed to increase our chances of reaching Grandma's house alive. Little Sis sat in the front seat with Mom and Dad. My brother JD sat in the middle seat next to all the food, and I was it the rearward-facing seat in back with all the luggage.

For years Mom told me that this was a special seat that not just anyone could use on a long trip. For example, they tried putting JD back there, and he got carsick before we even got out of town. This pretty much took the edge off that ride. So I was elected to hold down the luggage, and I never once puked. At the time, I thought of it as a major life achievement for a 10-year-old. Mom often commented on well I did in "way-back". Only later did I hear that Mom decided I needed to be in back because it was the best way to keep me and Dad as far apart as possible in such a small place. She was trying to avoid trouble, but all she did was move trouble to the back seat.

The rear set had one drawback- I had to crawl over all the food, my brother, and the luggage, but the way-back seat did have its perks. It gave me an interesting view of the world. I got to watch where we'd been and the satisfaction of knowing that we were leaving. This was a nice feeling when we were putting miles between us and a place like Bakersfield.  Since the back seat faced to the rear, everyone else in my family was facing the other direction and not paying all that much attention to me. I got to gawk at people who drove by, and I had a variety of games I used to play on tailgaters—people who got close enough to get a really good look.

One of my favorite things to do was to hold up a realistic toy gun and look at the driver menacingly. This caused some people to back off—mostly those with East Coast license plates. One time, though, a guy in a one-ton flatbed with Texas plates reached back and pulled his shotgun off the rack and sat it on his dash, the two barrels trained on me. He grinned, but he also followed us for mile after mile with that thing pointed at me.

That was the last time I did the pistol trick.

Still, there were other diversions. Another favorite pastime was to make signs and hold them up to the rear window. The signs might say helpful things like "Pass Carefully, Driver Chewing Tobacco." You could tell who believed this because they'd drop way back, and wait miles and miles for a passing lane. Other signs contained taunts: "We may Be Slow-But We're Ahead of You!" This often prompted just the opposite effect of the Chew-Signs, the driver would scowl, squint, and then pass in the face of oncoming traffic. They'd cut Dad off. This usually spurred an outpouring of colorful language from my father, who wanted to chase the offenders down, until my Mom restrained him and reminded him that an overloaded station wagon is not a police Interceptor. Still, Dad would yell: "Get That License Number!" But Mom never did.

The art of the back seat car sign is to hold it up long enough to be seen by the driver behind us but not by Dad in his rearview mirror or Mom during her periodic head count to see if someone had climbed onto the rear bumper.

I was the master of the sleight-of-sign, and my back-seat shenanigans were undetected for years, until I decided it would be fun to try something new.

Before this trip, my Mom fretted about a big story in the newspaper. Some crazy woman who wanted to have kids—but couldn't. Mom couldn't quit talking about it, and finally I asked her what "abducted" meant, and she said that it meant "kidnapped," when someone took a child that wasn't theirs without the parent's knowledge. Mom repeated her oft-told warning of not wandering off with strangers.

Dad wasn't worried. He'd tried to give me away a couple of time, but he'd had no takers. Even so, Mom took the precaution of stenciling our names and phone numbers in our underwear and jackets.

But this got me to thinking. It would be a great fun to make up a new sign that said: "HELP! I've been kidnapped. Call the police." This was a lot of information to write on one sign, and so the lettering was pretty small. I wasn't sure if kidnapped was one word or two, so I had to look it up it the dictionary I brought on the trip. I worked carefully with my crayons and markers to fit all the words on my cardboard sign, and I couldn't wait to try it out.

My first victim was a bald guy who was driving a pickup. He frowned for a minute, and then just laughed, waved, and honked as he drove by. I guess he figured out the gag.

Most of the other people I tried had similar reactions. Then I tried it on a white haired old lady driving a VW. She looked at the sign, and seemed confused. I saw her reach down in her purse and pull out a pair of glasses. She put them on, looked at me again, and looked startled. The head bobbed up and down as she nodded, and then made slashing downward motions with her hand, followed us closely to the next exit, and then peeled off. I lost sight of her as she dove into a gas station.

I decided that the sign was a bust, and lost interest. So, I picked up a Hardy Boys book, and burrowed down in the luggage to read for a while.

About 15 minutes later, something odd happened. I heard a siren, and I looked up to see not one, but two police cars boxed in our wagon, pulling us over.

Dad swore.

"What's wrong," Mom asked.

"Damned if I know." Dad said

The patrolmen advanced on both sides, guns drawn. Mom looked back and squealed.

"Don't move!" a cop yelled. And Dad didn't move. Then the officer looked at my brother, sister and I and frowned.

"Are you kids OK?" he asked.

"I have to go to the bathroom," Little Sis said. "I'm hungry," JD added. I realized what was happening, and slid the signs behind the ice chest. "I didn't do it," I said helpfully.

"Do what?" Mom asked, taking over the police work.

The cops lowered their guns, reassessing the situation.

"Step out of the car, please 'mam," said the officer nearest my Mom, holstering his weapon. The other stood in a strategic position, next to the driver's door. Dad sat silently and stared straight ahead, his jaw muscles pulsating.

The cop walked my mother to the back of the car, and she opened the tailgate at his direction. All my signs, wedged between the ice chest and the door, tumbled out on the ground at their feet. Mom looked at them, and then at me, wide-eyed.

The officer gathered up my messages. "Son, did you make these?" the he asked, his lips pursed.

"Yes sir."

There was a long silence. He scanned the car, looking us all up and down.

"Is this your mother?"

"Yes sir," I whispered.

The officer nodded his head and jerked his thumb towards the front of the car.

"And who is that man?"

I looked at my father. The other patrolman still had his gun in hand, and stood just inches from Dad. My father was facing him, hands-in-plain-view on the steering wheel. I could only see the back of Dad's head and neck, which were a bright red. I shifted my view to the rear-view mirror, and I could see the expression on his face. His mouth no longer had teeth, they were gritted fangs.

My voice failed me altogether.

The officer rested his free hand on his holster, which was still unsnapped.

"Son, you can tell me the truth," the officer cocked his head and rolled his eyes in a motion that made me look at Dad again. "Is this man your father?"

In the rear view mirror, I saw Dad's lips move. I couldn't hear what he was saying, but it didn't seem to be "I love you."

I drew a deep breath, but only a squeak came out. "I think so...."

The officer nodded, and waved off the other patrolman. I saw my father let go of the steering wheel, but his color changed from red to the sort of purple that Mom wore on Easter.

This didn't look good to me.

The patrolman bent down on one knee, and seemed twice as big up close. "So, son," he drummed his fingers on the signs and squinted at me. "Do you realize how serious this is?"

"I think so," I said, my voice still barely a whisper.

He leaned even closer, eyes fixed on mine, and waited. I exercised the right to remain silent. Then, Mother jumped in on my behalf.

"Oh, officer, I can assure you we'll take care of this," Mom said.

"DAMN STRAIGHT!" my father said, firing off his first words on the subject. "He'll get it, all right."

I shuddered.

The patrolman shuffled through my signs, reading each one in turn, nodding. I wasn't sure what I should be doing, so I studied his uniform. A shiny name-tag said "Thompson." Below, on his belt, I saw handcuffs. They, too, were shiny, and I wondered if they would hurt if he put them on me.

Officer Thompson clucked his tongue and straightened the stack of cardboard messages. He looked at me, his eyes dancing.

"And what do you have to say for yourself?" he asked, this time in a softer tone.

I felt my face turn red, and I studied my toes. "Sorry?" I said. I looked up again at officer Thompson and then my father who nodded his head curtly.

"Won't do it again?" the officer asked helpfully, biting his lip.

I shook my head. "No sir, never."

He put his face close to mine, and whispered, "Cross your heart?"

I silently crossed my heart, and for the first time, he smiled at me.

Officer Thompson stood up, looked at my father's contorted face in the mirror, and then leaned over near my mother and whispered in her ear.

"No, thank you. That won't be necessary," she said, and to my surprise, she smiled. "I'll take care of it."

"Very well, then," the patrolman nodded. "I don't think you'll need these anymore." He tucked the signs under his arm, and left.

Mom got back into the car, and then SHE whispered something in Dad's ear, and kissed him on the cheek. He frowned, and we drove onward in subdued silence.

I wasn't sure how to read the mood in the front seat. What was "it?" I had long heard Dad say "YOU'RE GOING TO GET 'IT.'" Mom had even promised the patrolman that she was going to take care of 'it.' Now, I was afraid, I was finally going to find out.

I hunkered down in the back seat, unable to read or do much of anything. It was a long, long way to the next gas station. I waited until Dad had gone inside to pay, and I scrambled over the seat to talk to Mom.

I sat down next to her and peered searchingly into her face.

"Do you need to use the restroom?" She asked nonchalantly.

"No."

"Well, then, you'd better get back in your seat."

"OK," but I lingered.

She looked at me, amused. "So…. what now?"

"Mom, what is IT?"

"It?"

"What did the policeman SAY TO YOU?"

"Oh, that." She smiled. "He was a bit worried about you…"

"Yeah?"

"He offered to take you into custody."

"Custody?" I was shocked. "He was going to arrest me?"

"No, love," she laughed, pinched my chin, and nudged me to return to the back seat. "He was offering 'protective custody.'"

# OH CHRISTMAS TREE!
# HOW NAKED
# ARE YOUR BRANCHES?

Oh Christmas tree, oh Christmas tree,

How naked are your branches

Oh Christmas tree, oh Christmas tree,

We sought you out, 'or many ranches


Not so long ago, we bundled you,

On the top, of Mom's Subaru

We brought you home,

    and Daddy-o

Stuck you in a bucket,

    on the back patio


Oh Christmas Tree oh Christmas tree

How naked are your branches

Our bulbs and bangles, sit next to you
But no one here, can find the time to
Hang lights, or garlands, or tinsel blue
It's really sad, but oh so true...

Oh Christmas tree, oh Christmas tree
How naked are, your branches

Your needles dry, and hit the floor
But little kiddies, dwell here no more
They used to clamor, to load you so
With stuff they made,
    from head to toe

Oh Christmas tree, oh Christmas tree
How naked are, your branches

Paper clips, tin foil and string
Play-Dough makes...
    strange-looking things

All sit in boxes, so near at hand

Memories of the Promised Land


Oh Christmas Tree, oh Christmas tree

How naked are your branches


We live in hope, that sometime soon

If not this morn,

    then perhaps by noon

Some once-small child,

    may drop in here

And take the pains,

    to spread some cheer


So gather round, brush 'way the dust

Drink some eggnog, if you must

Please open a box, do it for Mom

Put on the star, with joy and aplomb

And know that you, shall someday see

A tree like this, that'll be for thee

A memory of, the things change

And how the years do rearrange


Oh Christmas tree, oh Christmas tree

How naked are, thy branches


Our lives enriched, yet we sense loss

A space, a void, and some lichen moss

That lingers here,

    just out of sight

Adorn me please,

    before Christmas night


Oh Christmas Tree, oh Christmas tree

Bring one home,

    and take your chances

## YULE BE RICH!

"Can't we leave it up just a LITTLE longer, Mom?"

"No. It's browner than last week's bananas."

"PLEASE."

"No. It's a fire hazard."

"Chris still has his up."

"Chris has a plastic tree."

Mom had me there. It was true. And until this year, we'd always had a fake tree too. It took both Mom and me to talk Dad into a real tree.  He was against the idea from the start. After all, we had a "perfectly good" aluminum-tree with white flocking just waiting to go, complete with all-blue ornaments and small floodlights.

"There's nothing wrong with our tree," Dad said.

"Ronnie, It's time we had a real tree again."

"Too much work," Dad said.

"Ronald," Mom said.

"Too much money."

"Ronald James,"  Mom put her hands on her hips, and that was pretty much the end of that argument. Dad still complained about how our tinfoil tree still had "plenty of good years left in it." But all this was face-saving. We were driving to the lot, and the victory belonged to Mom and me.

She even let me pick out the tree. It was magical, a thing of beauty. To my seven-year-old mind, the tree was the best part of Christmas. I didn't want it to stop just because all the Christmas presents had been opened.

"Can't we just keep it?" I begged.

"Remember our understanding?" Mom said.

I sat there, lower lip protruding, hoping for a reprieve. Mom had made me all remove the lights, ornaments and the star. But the tinsel and pine-smell still made it feel like Christmas, even though it was well into January.

"Well," she tapped her foot.

"Yeah."

"No complaining this time?"

"I'm not complaining."

"You're fussing."

"But that's not complaining."

"It's irritating," Mom said, bending down a bit to look me in the eye.

"But Mom. It'll die outside."

"It's dead already, son."

"But we've watered it," I pointed to the basin at the bottom of the tree. "It's been drinking the water."

Mom shook her head, walked over to the bookcase and pulled volume "T" from the World Book. She flipped it open, and after a moment, pointed to a diagram of a tree, showing the roots.

"They cut it off at the roots. See?"

I looked at the diagram, unconvinced. I'd never seen roots. For all I knew, only some trees had them. Mom could be wrong. After all, our teacher broke parts off her potato plant, and it didn't die.

"Maybe they'll grow back."

"They won't," Mom said.

"My teeth do." I smiled broadly, showing a set of chompers in various stages of growth, decay and resurrection.

"Oh I give up," Mom finally said. "You can keep it, but take it outside, behind the garage. Just don't bother me with this tree business, OK?"

I said a big HURRAY, and with her help, dragged the tree outside. She returned to her work, and I planted it by the alley. It was then that I noticed that many neighbors had dumped their trees in the trash. I decided that I'd rescue those, too. I dragged them home, one by one, with my wagon. Each time I brought a tree, dug a hole, and crammed it in. Then, I packed the dirt and soaked the ground until it was nice and soft. I was working on the sixth tree when Chris dropped by and helped me.

"There's more over on my street," Chris said.

"We could plant them at your house."

Chris shook his head. "No room."

It was true. I still had plenty of space. We only had a half-dozen or so trees. But I was tired and sweaty from all the work. I wasn't sure I was up for the job.

"I don't know."

"Hey, do you want them all to die?"

"No." I hesitated, it was after all, three blocks to his house. "But it will take all day."

"We could use my new bicycle."

"Wow, you'd do that?" I was surprised. The bike was Chris' biggest-ever present.

"Sure, as long as I get half the profits."

"Profits?"

"Yeah, when we sell all these back next year. You'll be rich."

"Wow... Yeah." Chris was a genius. I'd been thinking about saving the trees. He'd seen a way to get rich. We'd show Dad that it truly was a great idea to get a real tree. "We should get going...."

"Before someone else gets 'em?" Chris completed my thought.

I paced off the space remaining, and figured we'd have room for zillions of trees.

"I wonder if we should charge extra for the ones that already have tinsel," I said.

"Or flocking, do you know how much Mrs. Young paid for hers?" Chris said.

"Maybe she's tossed it."

"Let's go check."

We took off, me dragging a Red Flyer and Chris taking inventory of all the trees we were passing on the way to his house.

"We're going to make a killing," Chris said.

"Yeah, and Dad can't complain about the cost."

And sure enough, when Dad got home and saw our farm of 17 trees, he didn't say a thing about the cost.

## TOYING WITH TROUBLE

Uncle Joe bought me my bazooka. He lived 3,000 miles away, in Detroit. I don't think he could hear the explosions, but I'm not sure. He quit calling us after Christmas.

That Sonic Blaster was one of two presents from my "Genius Uncle," as Mom called him. The other was the "Big Ear" eavesdropping dish. Mom confiscated it immediately. This seems an odd choice. You'd think that she'd have appreciated the peace and quiet afforded by "the Ear" over the Blaster's glass-rattling explosions.

My parents were remarkably patient people. But it took them a while to discover our fundamental philosophical difference. They thought that toys were supposed to be fun and buy them a few moments of peace. I thought that my toys were tools of discovery, or war, depending on where you stood.

Standing far away was usually a good idea.

Some of their gifts they soon regretted – toy saws that really cut wood, pocket knives and magnifying glasses. I blamed them. They were the adults, and it really was their fault when I torched leaves, incinerated bugs, or modified our furniture to better fit a family of Munchkins.

Take the "Bangsite Cannon." This 18-inch piece of artillery fell into my possession when I was 10. It used the same gas that fuels a cutting torch.

The cannon's operating instructions said to "put two teaspoons of water in the barrel. Dip plunger into 'Bang-site compound' available at toy stores everywhere! Insert assembly into breech, rotate, count to 10. Depress plunger smartly."

"Smartly" in this case, means rapidly; it does not reflect the wisdom of giving an explosive device to a hyperactive boy.

I loved the cannon. It made a bigger bang than grandpa's backfiring Studebaker. But soon the noise was just boooring. I looked at that barrel, and it wasn't enough just to *imagine* a shell flying from it into an enemy camp. It needed more oomph, so I applied "plaything-synergy." This is done by combining toys in unimagined, unintended, or forbidden ways.

I transformed my Tinkertoys, a sedate set of sticks, into missiles. Here's how it's done. Grab a stubby, a Tootsie-Roll-shaped cylinder, tack on a red tip for aerodynamics, and insert into the cannon's barrel... Voila! You've got an artillery shell.

The first volley was so-so. It flew over the house and bounced off the dog.

Further work was in order. In a short time, I discovered that TWO stubbies, connected with a yellow shaft, were the ticket. This setup had stability and heft. Better yet, it looked cool, and felt like a real weapon, one to strike fear in the hearts of our neighbors and other enemies.

Sadly the newer, bigger, better bombshell would barely go across the front yard. It did put a cool looking dent in Dad's old Chevy, but it needed more "go-power."

Father always said: "When all else fails, read the directions." And he was so right! Instructions are the place to look for innovative methods only dimly anticipated by the manufacturer. Just remember that they're *suggestions*, not hard-and-fast rules.

So, I saw, in big red type, a cautionary a note to "**NEVER USE MORE THAN ONE SCOOP OF THE BANGSITE SOLUTION**." There were words I didn't understand like "excessive gas"... "injury to the operator." But what caught my eye was the "risk of explosion."

Of course, we needed an *explosion*— that's what powered the moon shots! So I doubled the charge. It helped. Tripling worked even better. I was back in business.

Scientific advances, though, often have setbacks and misfortune. Bad luck, in this case, arrived in the form of my kid sister. She came. She saw. She ratted me out. Little Sis dragged Mom into the front yard in time to witness the full glory of triple-charged Bangsite power applied to multi-stage-Tinkertoy technology.

It was a beautiful sight, that missile streaking nearly a city block. But Mom freaked, and that was the end of my cannon. Grownups have pitifully little appreciation for novel ideas.

So somewhere out there in the Twilight Zone sits a shelf full of long lost toys. My beloved cannon rests next to all the other cool stuff that was taken to keep me from killing myself.

Did Mom do the right thing? Who knows. Letting me be could have led to a benign but helpful career in applied physics, demolition, or the infantry. But she meddled, and I became an English major. So instead I'm both dangerous *and* useless.

# GRANDMA!
# THAT'S CHEATING!

Grandma was always packin,' and rarin' to go. They lived several states away, so when they visited over the holidays it was a big deal. Grandma *came prepared*. She carried her own dice, and could, on occasion, shoot them straight and true. But usually they took an odd bounce. 'Bama couldn't help it. It was her '*Yahtzee* elbow.'

"Hey, 'Bama, that's cheating," my brother whined.

"No, hon, they just up and jumped on my arm," Grandma smiled.

"But you bumped them after they'd stopped."

"Did I? Well hush my mouth." Her eyes opened wide. "If you like, I could roll again."

So she did. A couple tumbled off the table. She grabbed both in mid-air, and held them up for us to see.

"Two sixes."

Mom cocked her head. "Really?"

"They were gonna be sixes."

Mom rolled her eyes. "Well you should work for the FBI."

"Maybe I do,"

"Then arrest yourself, scofflaw."

Grandma winked, and penciled in a zero. "Ah... Just funnin' ya,"

And fun she was. 'Bama had more trick shots than Minnesota Fats.

Yahtzee wasn't our family's only passion. We also were Monopolists, members of a cult that deprives you of sleep, strips your wealth, and lands you in jail. Once hooked, you're forced to find fresh recruits. It's not easy. I lost a few friends by confining them in a small room, spending hours on end passing 'Go,' until we fell into a stupor.

So usually it was just me and my brother, JD. Since I was older, and more "responsible," I got to be the banker. Having your hands on other people's money is the best part of the game. Once, I wanted to buy hotels but was short on cash. I hit upon a creative financing scheme that would have impressed Goldman-Sacs.

"How about the bank loans us both $5,000?"

"Why?" JD frowned.

"For... improvements."

"Hotels on Boardwalk? Right?'

"Could be." I said.

JD scowled. "And I'll land on them."

"But you'll have $5,000."

"Until I lose it."

"Yeah. Then I can pay the bank back, and you'll go bankrupt."

"That stinks." JD said.

"It's business, little brother, and I'm gonna take the cash, even if you don't."

"Better not!"

"Show me where it says I can't!" I waved the rule book in his face.

"I'm tellin'."

Mom was summoned. She scanned the instructions.

"Nope. Not allowed."

"Ah, Mom. You can divvy stuff up for a shorter game."

"At the start," Mom sighed. "You don't change rules halfway through."

"But they're *nice hotels*," I said. "It's progress."

Mom shook her head. "Playing by the rules builds character. Try it, you'll see." She left, and my brother flashed a grin.

"Told ya'," JD said.

"OK." I put the rule book at my side. "She said I had to play *by* them, not *with* them. Now, how about some cash?"

"MOM!"

\*\*\*

Yet Mom did have a point. Playing by the rules does offer many valuable lessons. *Life*, for example, lets you taste the sweetness of "revenge" and sample the sin of gambling. It's all there in the rule book. Sure, *Life* touts college and a career, but you can place side-bets and spin the wheel. It's a great way to end up in the poor house.

Games teach us about emotions, too. Take *Sorry*. I learned how to pulverize my kid sister and see her dissolve in tears. Then I had to comfort her and tell her I was *sorry* she'd lost. Really, though, I was *thrilled* I'd won. At age 12, winning was *it*. As my baseball coach said: "Show me a good loser, and I'll show you a loser."

I did embrace one "Life" lesson. I decided to attend college. There, Backgammon was the game of choice. I played it to decompress during study breaks. Then came marriage, graduation, and kids. Old, familiar board games from my childhood crept back into my life along with our little rug rats - *Candyland*, *Chutes and Ladders*, even *Sorry* …. But the fun began for real when the kiddos were old enough to play my favorite, *Scrabble.* It was a big moment. We divided up the tiles, and I laid down my first word in family competition.

"What's a 'snarfz,' Daddy?" my daughter asked.

"It's a rodent that lives in Namibia." I smiled, and pointed towards our *World Books*. "You should look it up."

Across the table, my wife cleared her throat. "Really?"

"Oh, all right." I shrugged, taking the tiles, and losing my turn. "Maybe there are snarfzs and we just haven't discovered them."

"We'll leave that to Dr Seuss." She then took her turn, laying down "fabric" next to "ate."

"Fabricate," she smiled, patting me on the arm. "Triple word... double letter... 52 points."

"Slick," I said.

"And by the book."

Yes, rulebooks and reason still reside with Mothers, Inc. But you can't fight genetics. Case in point. My son and his older sisters were playing hide-and-seek when the four of them piled into the kitchen.

"Joe's cheating," the girls said in three-part harmony. "He's tagged out, but he won't be 'it.'"

Joe shrugged. "No I'm not."

"Yeah-huh," the girls said.

"I was touching the tree." To prove his point, he held up a twig.

"I think they meant the trunk." I hid a smile.

"But they didn't *say* that."

Karin looked at me and shook her head. "That acorn didn't fall far from the tree."

"We don't want to play hide-and-seek with *him* anymore." The girls pouted. "We want a game with *real* rules."

"OK, OK." I nodded and pointed at the table. "How about some *Yahtzee*?"

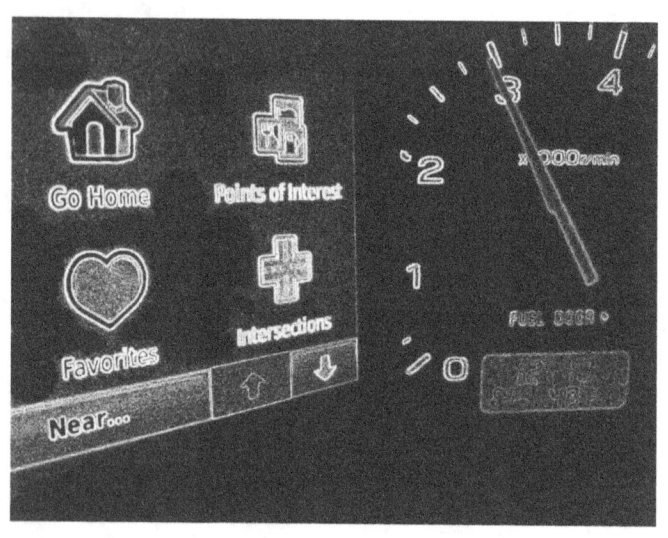

# DRIVING THROUGH
## THE SNOW
## DAD'S GPS
## AND
## "MISS DIRECTIONS"

Half of our holidays are spent on the road. Both my wife, Karin, and I have large families, and we're either traveling to see some sibling or entertaining them at our place.

As a group, we move around a lot, and so we're continually having to tell people, or be told, how to find our way over hill and dale. Since the days when cavemen had to find the convenience store without crossing the tar pits, we've all had to either give or receive directions. It's a skill, like kissing and telling jokes, that everyone **thinks** they do well.

Karin, and I can find our way around town without becoming fossilized, but when it comes to *giving* directions, we speak different languages.

She's a minimalist. Her instructions are brief, to the point, and work best if you already know how to get there. Karin disagrees, of course, but I've seen her directions, given to friends, on how to find our home.

"Turn left by the old Jacques' place, drive until you pass the barn that used to be red, count to ten, and then go south."

Clear? Yes, except the Jacques have moved—the mailbox now says "Anderson." The barn that *was* red comes after a barn that *is* red, and it's impossible to turn south from Old 44. When I mention this, she'll clarify, "well …. south-ish. OK?"

Her directions are easy to memorize. That's good, because you'll be driving a looooong time before finding us. Cal-Trans recently reported an upsurge in crop circles nearby caused by motorists endless looping off Highway 44.

My approach is to give fabulously-detailed directions. These include restaurant reviews, references to local history, scientific notes on area flora and fauna, and a rundown on road hazards and bad turns—the ones where our kids barfed. Insomniacs can read these notes and sleep for weeks. Friends see them and decide to stay home and just invite Karin over.

So our direction-giving is a competitive sport. After Karin gives her notes, I give mine. When our hapless guests finally arrive, I'll ask: "Which set was best?" The wise ones look at Karin, at me, and say both directions, *taken together*—work perfectly.

These days, though, the most common answer is: "Oh... Didn't need 'em, used GPS."

Alas... the art of giving directions is dying. And we're helping to kill it. Karin bought me a GPS for Christmas. She says the jury's still out on whether it was a good idea. It has added a new dimension to our trips. I punch in an address, press a button, and *Lizzie-from-London* takes over, we're off to a yard sale.

"In .5 miles, turn right on Old Alturas," says a clipped, British accent.

I'm about to make the turn, when a very familiar American voice countermands the direction.

"I wouldn't go that way," Karin says.

"Why not?"

"Rebecca's ex-boyfriend lives down there. He'll think you're checking up on him."

I have to decide in a flash which of the two women I'll obey.

I drive past the turn.

"Recalculating......" Lizzie says, sounding annoyed. "Turn right in .4 miles on Irene."

"Nope," Karin says.

"Why?"

"Don't ask."

The funny thing is, after years of marriage, this constitutes an explanation.

So, we pass turn after turn, irritating "Miss Directions," as my wife has come to call the "other woman." Eventually, all three of us reach our destination the way airlines do—taking a "Great Circle" route over the polar ice cap.

Karin hates my electronic playmate. Two summers ago, I was groping my way through a strange town, squinting at the GPS map, hanging on Lizzie's instructions. But something was amiss. After every turn, Lizzie had second thoughts, "recalculated," and told me do go back. We were going in not-so-great circles. Minutes ticked past, and our appointment loomed. All the while, Karin was sharing a story about one of her students, or the kids, or her dogs, I think. I really couldn't tell you. I was in the Traffic Twilight Zone, where there is **NO WAY TO GET THERE FROM HERE**, just like driving in Vermont.

Karin took control, breaking my trance, when she reached over and turned the GPS off.

"Hey," I said. "bring back Lizzie!"

"Really? You two have gone around the block three times," Karin said, unfolding a moth-eaten map. "Need help?"

"Yeah. Gimmie the GPS."

"Look. I've been finding our way for 20 years," Karin said. "I'll get you there."

"I don't want to be late," I said, reaching for the GPS. Karin held it out of reach.

"OK," I threw my hands up. "Just GET us there." I glanced at my watch. We had 10 minutes of "wiggle room." Karin studied her road atlas.

"Turn here, on the right," and she waved in a southeasterly direction. I pulled on the road.

"How far?"

"Just a bit," she said.

"A bit? Or a little bit?"

"Can't tell yet. I'll let you know." She held the atlas at arm's length, adjusted her glasses, and then slowly, when she thought I wasn't looking, turned the map right-side up.

"Might be faster to go left," she said.

"Where?"

"Back there a bit," she said, smiled, and hid her face behind the map. "Oops."

"You recalculating?" I asked.

"No," she said, looking me squarely in the eye. "I know *exactly* where I am."

"And that would be?"

"Sitting next to the guy who's got a *BIG DECISION* to make."

"What?"

She smiled. "Whether he's sleeping tonight with me…. or Miss Directions."

I stuffed Lizzie into the glove box, ending the affair.

We arrived in time, 10 minutes before Lizzie's best ETA…. by Karin's calculations….

And I'm not arguing with that.

# ABOUT THE AUTHOR

Robb Lightfoot has enjoyed writing and performing since he was a child, and many of his earliest performances earned him a special recognition-reserved seating in the principal's office at Highland Elementary. Since then, in addition to his weekly column on *aNewsCafe* - "Or So it Seems™" - Robb has written news and features for *The Bakersfield Californian*, appeared on stage as an opening stand-up act in Reno, and his writing has been published in the *Funny Times*. His work has won honorable mention in the *Writer's Digest* national short story competition, and his screenplay, "*One Little Indian*," vas a top-ten finalist.

The *Doggone Christmas* list is his first book, and his second collection, *The Stupid Minivan and More Stories of Midlife Madness* is available in both print and eBook form.

Robb presently lives, writes and teaches in Shasta County, Northern California. You may reach him at robb@robblightfoot.com